To: Sammy & Oliver

From: Papa & Nana

This book was made

B for **Baxter**

Story and Pictures by Ted Simonin

just for you × 2 &

Enjoy (!)

Ted Simonin

Brandylane
Publishers, Inc.
Publishing books since 1985

ISBN: 978-1-947860-20-9
LCCN: 2018955052

Printed in the United States of America

Published by

Brandylane Publishers, Inc.

Brandylane
Publishers, Inc.
Publishing books since 1985

To Carlos & Ilene

One day, Baxter was sitting in his backyard, thinking about how to build the ultimate ball-throwing machine, when he heard a voice calling his name.

"Baxter!" said the voice—and Baxter turned to see his friend Marcus land on the fence. "It's so nice to see you. I've brought someone I want you to meet. This is my sister, Fiona."

"It's nice to meet you, Baxter," said Fiona. "My brother has told me so much about you."

"We're getting ready to fly south," explained Marcus. "This time each year, we meet our parents at our family tree in Florida for our annual reunion."

"You're flying all the way to Florida for a family reunion? Sounds like fun! Count me in!" said Baxter.

Fiona glanced at her brother. "'Count me in?'" she whispered. "But Baxter's not part of our family!"

Then she turned and said loudly, "But Baxter, how will you get to Florida? You don't have wings to fly."

As quickly as he could, Baxter ran to his doghouse. He dove in headfirst, threw things everywhere, and pulled out . . .

BAXTER

. . . a state-of-the-art jetpack!

Baxter threw the jetpack over his shoulders and shot straight into the air. "Woohoo!" cried Baxter. "There's no better way to fly!"

"Come on, Fiona. Let's go!" Marcus said.

"Really, Marcus?! You're inviting a dog to our family reunion?!"

"Trust me, Fiona. Baxter's not just some dumb dog. You will grow to love him, I promise!"

And with those words, Baxter and the
two birds took to the sky.
They flew over mountains and valleys
and trees, and a few days later . . .

"Look!" said Marcus. "There's the Grand Canyon!"

"Marcus and I stop here every year," said Fiona. "It's a family tradition. Last year, we found a piece of driftwood and floated down the river all day long."

"You floated down the river?" said Baxter. "I have an idea. Let's land!"

Baxter and the two birds flew to the ground and landed next to the Colorado River.

As quickly as he could, Baxter unzipped the zipper on his jetpack, reached deep inside, and pulled out . . .

. . . a large raft with three paddles!

"Who wants to go rafting?" asked Baxter.

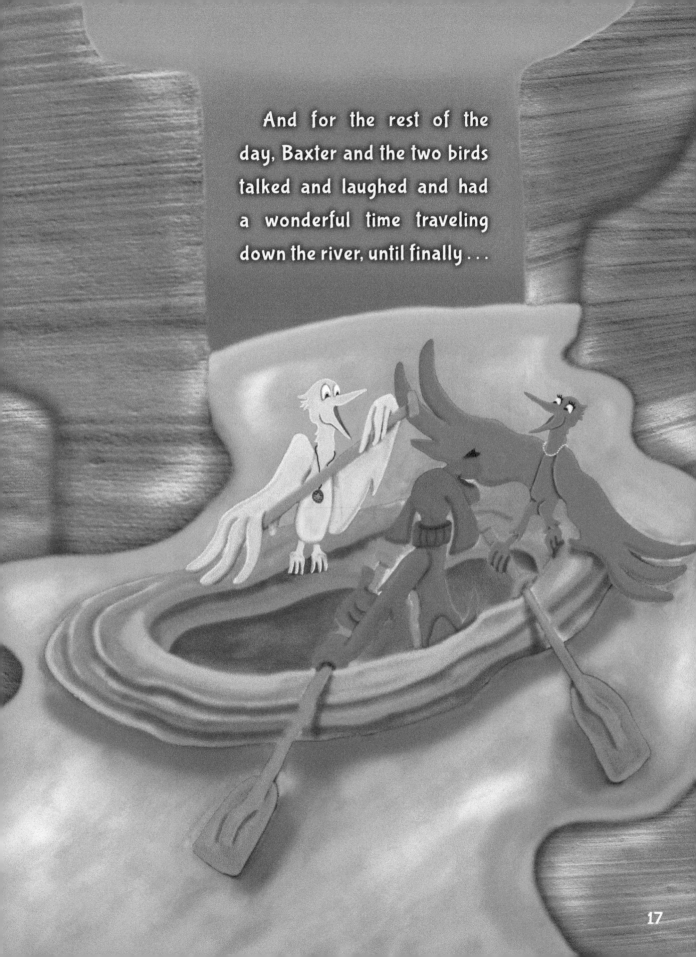

And for the rest of the day, Baxter and the two birds talked and laughed and had a wonderful time traveling down the river, until finally . . .

. . . Marcus and Fiona landed on a nearby tree, and Baxter plopped down on the ground. "Baxter, how did you fit that raft into your jetpack?" asked Fiona.

"It was easy," said Baxter. "I scanned it with the light rays from my supersonic shrinking machine. If you'd like, I'll show it to you when we get home."

"I'd like that," said Fiona. And with those words, the three of them fell fast asleep.

18

The next morning, Baxter and the two birds took to the sky again. They flew over rivers and fields and dirt—covered roads, and a few days later . . .

"Look!" said Marcus. "There's the city of New Orleans!"

"Marcus and I always stop here, too," said Fiona. "Last year, we listened to live jazz music in the streets for hours and hours!"

"Live music?" said Baxter.

"I have an idea. Let's land!"

Baxter and the two birds flew to the ground and landed on Bourbon Street.

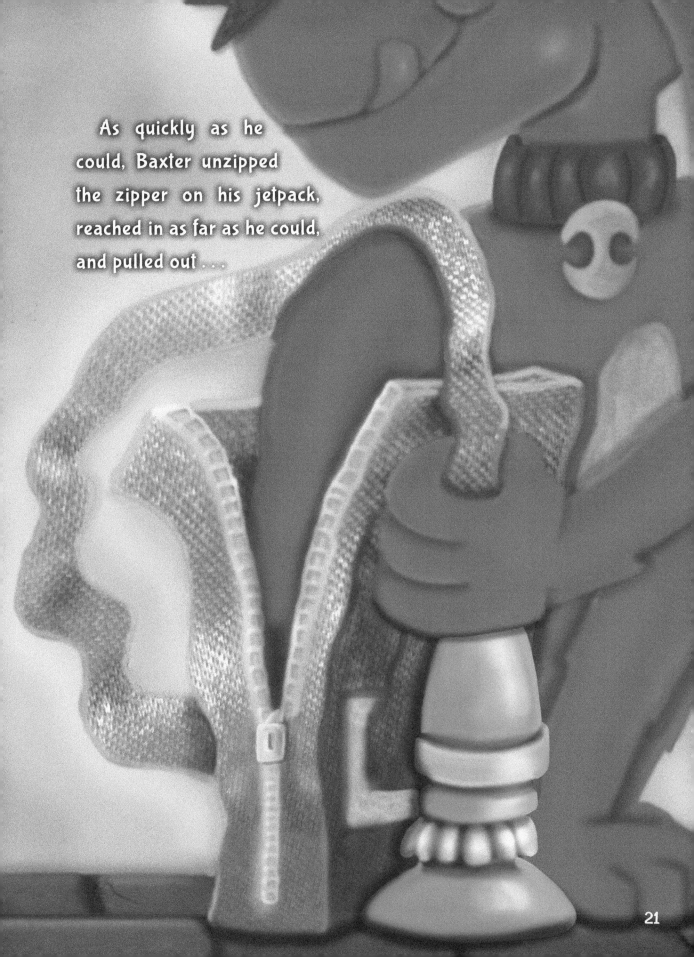

As quickly as he could, Baxter unzipped the zipper on his jetpack, reached in as far as he could, and pulled out . . .

21

. . . a piano,
a saxophone,
and a trumpet!

"Who wants to make some music?" asked Baxter. And for the rest of the day, Baxter pounded on the keys of the piano, Fiona poured her heart into the saxophone, and Marcus blew every last breath into the trumpet. The three of them had a grand old time, until finally . . .

. . . Marcus and Fiona landed on a nearby tree, and Baxter plopped down on a patch of grass.

"Baxter, where did you learn how to play the piano like that?" asked Fiona.

"It was easy," said Baxter. "I have a baby grand piano in my doghouse, and I practice every day. If you'd like, I'll show it to you when we get home."

"I'd like that," said Fiona.

And with those words, the three of them fell fast asleep.

The next morning, Baxter and the two birds took to the sky again. They flew over water and beaches and gator–filled swamps, and a few days later . . .

"Look!" said Fiona. "We made it! There's our family tree!"

Baxter and the two birds flew to the ground. They looked around for Marcus' and Fiona's family, but soon realized no one was to be found.

"That's odd," said Fiona. "They always meet us here every year!"

Suddenly, Baxter spotted a square piece of wood not far from the tree. "Look!" He picked it up and gave it to Marcus.

Marcus closely examined the piece of wood. "It's a note from Mom and Dad!"

Dear Marcus and
Fiona,

The Pelicans invited
us to a wedding
on the eastern shore
and we all went together.
We'll be back early
on Saturday.
Love, Mom, Dad,
& the whole family

"Thank goodness you found that note, Baxter!" said Fiona.

Suddenly, Baxter noticed something carved into the bark of the tree. He moved closer to get a better look.

"What are all these words carved into the branches?" asked Baxter. As he moved closer, he noticed something special about the words.

"Wait a minute," he said. "They're all names!"

"Fiona does all the carving," explained Marcus.

"That's right!" Fiona said proudly. "I've got the pointiest beak in the whole family.

Ethel

Michael

George

Sue Ann

Jonathan

Fiona

Marcus

Kiko

Lois

Raymond

I can carve a name into a tree faster than a woodpecker! Look at this." Fiona flew to a branch.

Arthur

Patrick

Kayla

Carlos

Barbara

Lisa

Hannah

29

"Here's my name, F–I–O–N–A. And here's M–A–R–C–U–S. And L–O–I–S. That spells my mother's name, And here's my father, R–A–Y–M–O–N–D.

Fiona

Marcus

Lois

Raymond

Wow!" said Baxter.
"You weren't kidding.
This really is a family tree!"

Michael

Ethel

George

Sue Ann

Jonathan

Marcus and Fiona helped Baxter read every name on the tree. Finally, the two birds landed on different branches and Baxter plopped down on a patch of grass.

Fiona

Marcus

Lois

Kiko

Raymond

"I can't wait for you to meet the rest of our family, Baxter!" said Fiona.

"I know!" said Baxter. "After reading all their names, I feel like I know everyone already!"

And with those words, the three of them fell fast asleep.

Arthur

Patrick

Kayla

Carlos

Barbara

Lisa

Hannah

31

That night, Baxter found himself tossing and turning. The next morning, he awoke with a tremendous yawn.

"Are they building a highway or something?" he asked. "I kept hearing a jackhammer, or some sort of—"

But before Baxter could finish what he was saying, he glanced up at the tree and noticed the letter B. Then he noticed the letters A—X—T—E—R.

"That spells 'Baxter'!" he said to himself. He looked up into the tree, and saw Fiona smiling. And when Baxter realized what Fiona had done . . .

Fiona

Marcus

Baxter

Lois

Raymond

. . . he gave her the
BIGGEST
hug there ever was!

33

About the Author and Illustrator

Ted Simonin, originally from Niagara Falls, New York, attended the University of Buffalo and finished with a master's in English. After graduation, Ted moved to the south of France, where he devoted himself to a daily routine of drawing, painting, and writing. His surroundings, coupled with a great discipline to create, inspired him to develop his unique style of illustrating and storytelling. Ted's work has been featured in *Highlights* and appeared in a literary journal for the Bob Dylan Music Festival, and his lighthearted character Baxter has been applauded by young readers across the country. Ted is a member of the Society of Children's Book Writers & Illustrators and now lives with his family of four in Fort Lauderdale, Florida.

"Ted is a big supporter of the Best Friends Animal Sanctuary in Kanab, Utah, a sanctuary that provides a home for more than 1,600 homeless animals. For more information please visit http://bestfriends.org."

—Best Friends Corporate Relations (corporaterelations@bestfriends.org)

(sent by dianef@bestfriends.org)

CPSIA information can be obtained
at www.ICGtesting.com
Printed in the USA
BVHW02*1710131018
529453BV00003B/6/P